For information regarding permission, write to:
Disney Licensed Publishing
114 Fifth Avenue, New York, New York  10011.

ISBN 0-7172-6811-X

Designed and produced by Bill SMITH STUDIO.

Printed in the U.S.A.
First printing, January 2004

# Try to See It My Way

*A Story About*
*Empathy*

by **Jacqueline A. Ball**
illustrated by
**S.I. International**
and
**Teresa Lester**

## SCHOLASTIC INC.

**New York   Toronto   London   Auckland   Sydney**
**Mexico City   New Delhi   Hong Kong   Buenos Aires**

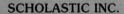

"What a perfect day for doing the laundry!" Briar Rose exclaimed. "Our clothes will dry quickly in all this sunshine."

$\mathcal{M}$erryweather added an apron to the laundry basket. "Thank you, dear."

"You're welcome, Aunt Merryweather," Briar Rose replied. "Aunt Fauna? Aunt Flora? Do you have any laundry for me to take to the stream?"

$\mathcal{F}$lora, Fauna, and Merryweather weren't really Briar Rose's aunts. They were good fairies, secretly raising her in the forest. Briar Rose was really the Princess Aurora. But she didn't know any of that.

"Here are some hankies, dear," said Fauna.

"We'll start the spring cleaning while you're gone, Briar Rose," Flora said. "There are so many old things I'm just itching to throw away."

Merryweather sighed.

Briar Rose blew them a kiss. "When I come back, I'll make lemon custard for a special treat."

After Briar Rose left, Flora and Fauna got busy. They carried out armloads of broken and unused things and dumped them into a big pile.

"Just look at this rubbish," said Flora. "Why would anyone keep this clutter around?"

$M$erryweather picked up each item they put down. "Briar Rose used to put flowers she picked for us in this vase. And look! Here's the comb we used for her hair."

She brushed away a tear. "Why would anyone want to throw away such memories?"

Finally, Flora and Fauna dragged out an old, broken chair. "All done!" Flora called happily. "Now we can clean the floors!"

She went back into the cottage.

$\mathcal{M}$erryweather plopped down into the chair, wiggling her bottom until she was comfortable. "They don't make chairs like this anymore, Fauna," she said sadly.

"There, there, Merryweather," said Fauna.

"Come on," Flora called from the doorway.
"Time to sweep and wash the floors."

"*I*n a minute," Merryweather answered, leaning her head back on some old pillows. Feathers puffed out in a cloud. All these things were special. How could she keep them from being thrown away?

Suddenly she smiled. "I have an idea," she said. "Will you help me, Fauna?"

*A* little while later, Merryweather and
Fauna joined Flora in the kitchen. "Now, how
can we help?" Merryweather asked brightly.

"How about cleaning off these shelves, while
I find the scrubbing brush?" Flora suggested.

$\mathcal{A}$s Flora searched another shelf, two chipmunks scurried out from behind some clutter. She gently guided them out of the door, and Merryweather tossed them some bread crusts.

"Where could that scrubbing brush be?" Flora muttered quietly.

*F*lora thought for a minute. "Maybe it's in the back closet."

Fauna and Merryweather exchanged panicked glances.

"Uh, I'm sure the scrubbing brush isn't there, Flora," Merryweather said nervously.

"Don't waste your time," added Fauna.

But Flora was already at the closet door.

"*H*mm," said Flora. "Something about this closet looks funny." She peered closely. "Feathers? What on earth?"

"No, no!" exclaimed Merryweather.
"Don't open that door, Flora!" called Fauna.
It was too late. Flora yanked the door open.

*F*lora leaped back just in time. The pile of things that had been outside before tumbled out of the closet. The old chair barely missed her big toe!

"Good heavens!" cried Flora.

Merryweather and Fauna looked down.

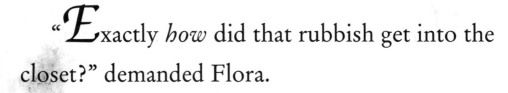

"*E*xactly *how* did that rubbish get into the closet?" demanded Flora.

"I carried it in through the window," Fauna confessed.

Merryweather lifted her chin. "It was my idea," she answered. "And it is *not* rubbish!"

"*It is* rubbish!" said Flora. "And out it goes—again!" She scooped up the chair and several items and carried them back outside.

Merryweather ran after her. "Then in it will come—again!"

Fauna just didn't know what to do.

When Briar Rose returned, she couldn't believe her eyes. As fast as Flora carried things out of the cottage, Merryweather took them back inside. "What is going on?" Briar Rose asked.

"Merryweather refuses to throw this worthless, old stuff away," said Flora angrily.

"For the last time, it is *not* worthless!" Merryweather protested.

$\mathcal{B}$riar Rose was worried. She knew that Flora and Merryweather loved each other. She knew how kind they both were, and that they didn't enjoy fighting. How could she make each of them see the other's point of view?

# What would a princess do?

"Please, stop for a moment and tell each other why you're upset," Briar Rose said.

"Flora is being bossy, as usual," said Merryweather. "She wants everything her way!"

"You're the one who wants everything *your* way!" retorted Flora.

"You all taught me that everyone sees and feels things differently," Briar Rose said softly. "You explained that *empathy* means imagining how someone else feels." Then she looked at her two aunts lovingly. "Now I think you need to try to see things through each other's eyes."

The three fairies were silent.

$\mathcal{F}$inally, Merryweather said, "Well, why do you *have* to clean all the time, Flora?"

"Because it makes me happy to have a nice clean house," Flora answered. "Cleaning is my way of showing you that I care about you."

"That's why you sweep under our beds and shine our shoes whenever we're sad," Fauna explained quietly.

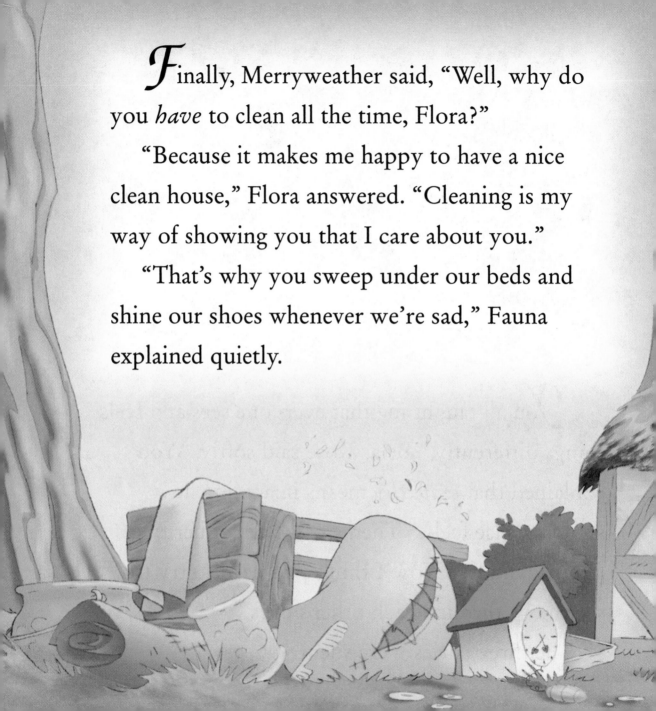

*T*hen Flora asked Merryweather, "Why do you want to keep worn-out, broken, old things?"

"Because things that remind me of the past make *me* happy," Merryweather replied.

"Remember how she cried when we threw out that old cake pan?" said Fauna.

"I baked Briar Rose's first birthday cake in that pan," said Merryweather.

"I remember," said Flora softly.

Flora put her arm around Merryweather. "There isn't room for everything, but would it make you happy to save a few of these things and keep them in the closet?"

$\mathcal{M}$erryweather nodded. "I'll pick out the most special ones. And I promise to step into your shoes once in a while, Flora."

"Just don't hide them in the closet!" laughed Briar Rose. "Now, I'm going to make lemon custard. That's something everyone can agree on!"

$\mathcal{T}he\ End$